Fondness for the Baker

Book Two

Small Town Matchmaker

Cheryl Wright

Fondness for the Baker
(Book Two, Small Town Matchmaker)

Copyright 2023 by Cheryl Wright

Small Town Romance Publications

Dedication

To Margaret Tanner, my very dear friend and fellow author, for her enduring encouragement and friendship.

To Alan, my husband of over forty-eight years, who has been a relentless supporter of my writing and dreams for many years.

To You, my wonderful readers, who encourage me to continue writing these stories. It is such a joy knowing so many of you enjoy reading my stories as much as I love writing them for you.

Table of Contents

Chapter One

Crystal Springs, Montana – 1880s

Martha Cooley wiped her brow on her sleeve. The heat from the stove was almost overwhelming.

She should be used to it. After all, she'd been working in the diner since Beth had left to have her baby.

Sweet Elijah, such a wonderful child.

The thought left Martha longing for a child of her own. With Beth and Wyatt marrying so late in their lives, and having a baby no less, it gave her hope. Of course, a husband needed to be involved, and for her, that was the missing element.

"Will you be right for a while, Allie?" Martha asked her kitchen assistant. "I need some fresh air."

Alison Hubertson stared at her. "Are you alright?" Of course Allie would worry about her. She was a kind and caring person.

"I am, I promise. I've been standing over that stove for hours, and the heat is getting to me."

Allie scowled. They both knew Martha was used to the heat. Why today would be different, she did not know. Hopefully, she wasn't coming down with something. She accepted the water Allie offered and went outside without another word. The fresh air would do her good, she was certain.

As she sat on the wooden bench situated outside the diner, Martha took deep breaths. The clean air really was refreshing. She was already beginning to feel better.

"Good morning," Joel Evans called from across the street. Standing outside the mercantile, he hesitated, then stepped toward her. "Are you feeling alright? You're pale."

Martha slapped her hands to her face, hoping to put some color into her cheeks. "The heat was a bit much today," she told her friend. "You know how that goes." As the town baker, Joel could surely relate, although he had been baking far longer than Martha had been working at the diner. Until the injury to Beth's arm that prevented her from working in the diner for some time, Martha had only worked there occasionally.

Best friends for many years, they'd become even more so since Sheriff Wyatt Holt came on the scene. Joel was a friend of Wyatt's. And he was Martha's friend, too. Until the town matchmaker had tried to push them together, there was a time she thought it might be more.

Martha shook herself mentally. That was all water under the bridge now. She and Joel had parted ways as friends, and were still friends.

"Do you need a doctor?" Joel asked, concern creasing his face. "I can fetch Marcus."

Martha brushed his fears aside. "The fresh air is helping. It's been busy already this morning. The stage is coming through tomorrow, and you know what that's like. I was getting ready for that, as well as doing today's prep."

Joel nodded his head. He had customers from the stage too, but from what Martha understood, they bought from the bakery in case they got hungry along the way. The diner was where most of the travelers headed.

"As long as you're sure." He pierced her with his gaze. "I'll be back later to check on you," he said, studying her again.

Martha nodded. She didn't want Joel wasting his time on her—it was a minor setback, that was all. She sipped the water Allie had given her, then stood. Unsteady on her feet, she sat down again.

"Let me get Doc Ryan," he pleaded, but again, Martha waved him away.

"I got overheated, that's all." She stared up at him and smiled tentatively. Unfortunately, Joel knew her far too well.

He sat down beside her. "I'm not leaving until you feel better." He was a stubborn man, but she appreciated his friendship. "Stop scowling," he told her firmly. "Friends look out for each other."

That made Martha chuckle. They sat together for the next ten minutes, and when she felt better, she went back inside. Joel followed her.

"You need some air in here," he said, inspecting the kitchen. "Keep this door open while you're cooking, Martha," he said, a scowl on his face. "You should know better. You've been working here for a long time now. If you don't want to open the door, at least raise the window a bit."

"It's stuck," Allie told him.

Joel strolled over to the window and could not move it. "Where's Wyatt's toolbox?" he asked.

Allie leaned down and passed over the toolbox. Joel selected the tools he needed, then set about fixing the window. "Now you can open it," he said with a smile.

"For that," Allie said, "you get a slice of Martha's famous cake."

Joel grinned. Martha knew how much he loved her cakes—he would occasionally have coffee and cake at the diner. She wasn't sure if that was because he was hungry, or to spend time with her. "You don't have to do that," he said, sounding slightly annoyed. "Friends help each other with no expectation of reward." Despite his protests, Allie handed him a plate with a slice of lemon cake.

"Find a seat and I'll bring you coffee," Martha's assistant told him firmly.

Joel grinned. "Perhaps I should fix the window more often." He chuckled then. "But honestly, I didn't expect anything in return."

"We know," Martha said, a smile on her face, "but it's the least we can do." Joel shrugged his shoulders and moved out to the dining room. Martha was not far behind him. It wasn't long before she joined him at the table. Allie placed a mug of coffee in front of him shortly afterwards. "What happened to us, Joel?" Martha asked quietly, trying not to let Allie hear the conversation.

He stopped eating and glanced up at her. "Dennis happened. If you recall, neither of us wanted to be manipulated by our *dear* mercantile owner."

Martha remembered. The memory had never left her. With Wyatt and Beth courting and then getting married, not to mention having a baby, it all came to the surface again. "Why did we let his actions separate us?" Martha suddenly felt irritated with herself, not to mention Joel. There had been a time where they were almost inseparable. The moment Dennis interfered and told everyone in town they were a couple, things soured between them. Things had never been the same since.

Joel lifted his coffee mug and took a long drink. As she studied him, Martha knew he was considering his answer. "Maybe we just weren't meant to be," Joel said, as he shrugged again. "I truly don't know."

"I don't know either," she said sadly. They were happy together back then, but letting Dennis, who was known as the town matchmaker, rule their lives was a foolish move. They both knew it to be true.

Swallowing down the last of his coffee, Joel stood. "Thanks for the cake and coffee," he said as he headed toward the door. "I should get back. Anyway, we're still friends, so that's the main thing."

Was it really? Martha stared after him as Joel left the diner, wondering if what he said was true. Not that she particularly wanted any sort of relationship, but the pair had been happy together. If either of them didn't marry soon, it would be too late. Just because it had worked for her friends, Beth and Wyatt, didn't mean it would work for her. Martha did not want to leave it too long to find her chance at happiness.

If Joel was no longer interested, she might have to look elsewhere.

Chapter Two

Joel headed back to the bakery, feeling upset over his conversation with Martha. Why were they allowing Dennis to derail their lives? Weren't they entitled to be happy? Apart from the fact there were far more men in town than women, he and Martha liked each other.

In his mind, it was more than a mere friendship. He really enjoyed Martha's company and would do anything for her. They were both considered past their prime, but Wyatt and Beth were living proof that age meant nothing if two people were truly in love.

The thought made him pause. Were they in love? He really wasn't sure. They certainly enjoyed each other's company, and they didn't rile each other up. They also agreed on things most of the time. When Dennis had interfered and told anyone who would listen they were together and would marry soon, things soured between them.

It was both their faults. They should not have allowed Dennis to rule the roost in their relationship. He knew Martha was furious with Dennis, and from what he could tell, upset about the entire affair. They had been courting for some time, and he was on the verge of asking her to marry him.

All that changed with Dennis spreading word around Crystal Springs. Fury rose up inside him at the thought. He still had a soft spot for Martha. In fact, it had never left him. He looked out for Martha, and had done so even before they began courting.

"If you're done woolgathering," Mrs. Hargreaves said, "I will take that carrot cake."

The customer's words pulled Joel back to the present. "Of course, Mrs. Hargreaves. I apologize." He quickly wrapped it in brown paper and handed it over. The woman handed him the money and harrumphed, then strode out of the store.

What was he thinking? Far too much, Joel decided. He needed to get his mind back on his bakery business and stop worrying about things past. There were plenty of other women in town. He would check things out and decide what to do. He was turning forty soon—Joel couldn't afford to wait much longer if he wanted to produce an heir.

He mentally ran through some of the available women in town. There was Ethel, the schoolma'am, or Alice, who was the dressmaker. Or perhaps Allie. Joel shook himself mentally. That would never do.

How could he court the woman right under Martha's gaze? No, that definitely wouldn't do.

His choices were few and far between. Joel decided to give it more thought. His heart thudded. The woman he really wanted to be with was Martha. There was no substitute.

"Ah, Mrs. Cavendish," he said, sounding delighted. He was far from thrilled to see this fussy customer, but put on a brave face since she was a regular. "I'll take your last carrot cake and half a dozen blueberry muffins," she said, handing over some notes. "Keep the change," she said once she had her package. It was always nice to get a generous tip.

"Thank you and good afternoon to you, Mrs. Cavendish," Joel said, opening the door for his best customer. He glanced diagonally across the road, trying to catch a glimpse of Martha, but she was nowhere to be seen.

He felt like a schoolboy with his first love. Joel was far from that, but still his heart fluttered when the diner door opened and Martha hurried across the road to the mercantile. It was all he could do not to rush over to her.

Why did he go to her this morning? It had triggered a lot of memories, all of them good. He wondered if he should go to the mercantile and check if she needed help to carry her supplies. If he did, would

Martha be mad at him? Would she think he was watching her every move?

Not only would it be wrong, but it could intimidate Martha. He wasn't one of those men who followed women and scared them. He was in love with her and wanted to spend more time with her.

Whether or not that happened was a completely different thing.

Joel began baking around five in the morning each day, so it was a long day for him. The store was usually closed by three. He had contemplated getting someone to run the counter sales for him, but thought about the money. There were a few young women in town who would fit the bill. But did he want to spend money on wages when he could do it himself?

His mind immediately went to Mrs. Cavendish. She had a daughter in her mid-twenties. As far as Joel was aware, Molly was living at home and still single. Did that mean she was available to work?

There was a time Molly had left town to attend finishing school. Why on earth anyone living in Crystal Springs would send their daughter somewhere like that was beyond his comprehension.

He shook the thought away. Right now, Joel could cope. He was always asleep early—it was a habit he'd had for most of his adult life. As an apprentice baker in Helena, he learned early to bed was the best option. He had never wavered from the habit.

With no customers in the store, Joel headed toward his large kitchen and cleaned up. He liked everything to be spotless and ready for the next day. Most of the bread pans were already clean, as were the trays. He wiped down the kitchen benches, swept the floor, then checked the ovens were cool enough for him to clean them too. At this time of day, they usually were.

He returned to the store when he heard the door open. "Afternoon, Joel," Dennis, the mercantile owner, said. "I've come to put in an additional order."

Joel raised his eyebrows. "Business good then?" As the mercantile's sole supplier of baked goods, Joel had pondered whether it was a good business decision. He'd concluded long ago that making exclusive products for the mercantile, and charging a premium price, was good for him, as well as Dennis.

The other man laughed. "It's those custard pastries you make. My customers love them. I'd like to increase the order by half again on the days the stagecoach is in town."

Now it made sense. Joel's custard pastries were quite delicious, and a handy snack for travelers. "Of course," he said cheerfully. "It's too late for today, though."

Dennis looked disappointed. "I should have realized that. Alright, if you can start next week, I'd be grateful." He was about to turn away when a sly look covered his face. "I saw you with Martha this morning. How is she doing?"

Joel's heart thudded. He hoped Dennis wasn't back at his matchmaking antics again. "She was feeling a little unwell and needed air. Overheated," he added, ensuring Dennis didn't start spreading rumors. The man was the town gossip and favored himself as a matchmaker, and neither sat well with Joel.

"I'm sorry to hear that," Dennis said. "Give her my best when you see her again." He fought back a grin, and Joel knew he was up to his old tricks.

Normally, he would keep information close to his chest, but this time, he wanted to stop Dennis before he began gossiping. "I fixed the window in the diner's kitchen. She should be fine now."

"Good," Dennis said, then left without another word.

Joel was furious. Dennis and his mercantile might be his most reliable customer, with daily sales, but the man was a pest. Sheriff Tommy Garrett should have a talk with Dennis and ban him from rumor-mongering. Wyatt would never have allowed it to continue.

He was still deep in his thoughts about the terrible side of Dennis Andrews that frustrated everyone so much when the bell over the door tinkled.

"Wyatt, I was just thinking about you," Joel said.

The former sheriff chuckled. "I saw Dennis leaving." A grin covered his face.

Joel never had to pretend with his friend and rolled his eyes. "The man is incorrigible. I'm sick of his matchmaking ways." He sighed and Wyatt stared at him.

"Beth and I would not have got together if it wasn't for Dennis," Wyatt said. "And look how that turned out. Speaking of Beth, she has a hankering for something sweet."

Joel winced. "Pregnancy cravings?"

"You guessed it," Wyatt said. "I don't want her to overdo it, and insisted she was not to bake. What do you have left at this late hour of the day?"

Joel glanced about. "Carrot cake and lemon cake. If you'd been here an hour earlier, I had far more on offer."

"I'll take the carrot cake, please. Beth likes that." Wyatt pulled out his wallet.

"I have one cupcake left. I'll throw that in at no charge for Elijah," Joel said. He would likely end up throwing it away or eating it himself. He'd rather give the young boy a bit of happiness.

"Thank you, Joel. Elijah will love that."

Warmth flooded Joel. The mere act of doing something good for another person was so heartwarming. He placed the cake and cupcake in a paper bag and handed them over. "By the way, I loosened the kitchen window at the diner today. It was stuck and Martha was getting overheated."

Wyatt's head shot up. "Thank you. I'll check it out. Those ladies work hard—I won't have them uncomfortable or ill as a result. I'll be heading there after I drop these home. Stagecoach day," he said, and Joel fully understood. Sometimes the travelers were rowdy, and other times they tried to leave without paying. Wyatt ensured there was no trouble for the two women working at the diner alone.

He was happy to help—anything to keep Martha and Allie safe.

After Wyatt left, it got Joel thinking. Again. He'd known Wyatt since he arrived in Crystal Springs, and his friend had been far happier since he and Beth had got together. They had kept apart for two whole years before they finally gave in to their feelings. Dennis and his interfering ways didn't help them, either.

He shook his head. Joel knew he had to decide. Either he went with his heart and pursued Martha, or he gave up on her completely.

As he locked up for the day, Joel made his decision. Martha was in his heart, and he wouldn't give up on them. Now he had to devise a way to win her back.

Chapter Three

With the stage coming through today, Martha arrived early. As she strolled past the bakery, she glanced inside to check if Joel was there. She hoped he wouldn't see her, but she was mistaken. His head shot up, and he waved. The next thing she knew, Joel was out on the street greeting her.

"Good morning," he said, brushing flour from his hands. His white apron was covered in flour. Martha knew how that went—she always began the day with a crisp white apron, but before the lunch service even began, it needed changing.

"Good morning to you too," she said, then, without thinking, reached out to brush the flour from his cheek. She pulled her hand back, but he clasped her wrist, then leaned into her hand. "Joel," she said slowly, not wanting to finish the words. They were done. They'd had their chance at love and it hadn't worked out.

He suddenly dropped her hand. "You're right, I'm sorry," he said, his eyes suddenly sad. "I guess I was hoping…" He shook his head then, and Martha felt his sadness. She, too, had hoped they would get back together.

She swallowed hard. "I… I should go," she said, then hurried away before he could utter another word. Joel's gaze seemed to burn a hole in her back. No matter what, she would not turn to see if he was still there. They needed to keep away from each other, but in a town the size of Crystal Springs, it was difficult.

Allie was waiting outside the diner door by the time Martha arrived. She felt breathless, which was ridiculous. There was no reason for it, except…

"I saw you talking to Joel," Allie said, trying to force back a smile. "Are you two together again?"

Martha glared at her. "No!" she said far too quickly. "Sorry. Joel would like it to be that way." She unlocked the door, and the pair went inside.

"What about you, Martha? What would you like?" Allie studied her, not taking her eyes away from Martha's face for even a moment. It was unnerving.

"Honestly?" Martha said. "I'm not sure. When we parted, it broke my heart. I don't think I could go through that again."

"Who says you will? If you don't try, you'll never know." Allie reached for the aprons and handed one to Martha, then put her own apron on. "It's obvious you like each other."

Martha closed her eyes momentarily, then turned away. "It goes deeper than that," she whispered. Tears filled her eyes for all she had lost. She hurried into the pantry, ensuring Allie didn't witness her weakness.

When she returned, arms full of flour, sugar, and other essentials, Allie was standing at the kitchen counter, waiting for her. "Why don't you just tell Joel how you feel?"

Her words shocked Martha. How could Allie be so naïve as to think a woman could tell a man she loved him? Particularly when he hadn't said it first.

It was different when the man was your husband, but not when you weren't married to him. She shook her head. "That wouldn't be right," Martha said quietly, then prepared for the day's menu. It would be busy today, with the stagecoach passengers coming, and she needed to get started.

Allie reached for the large bowl Martha needed to make pastry. "What can I do to help?" she whispered.

Martha stared at her. "Grab the butter and eggs? I forgot those earlier." That wasn't what Allie meant, and she knew it, but the conversation was making Martha's heart ache. Besides, she wanted to move on. Even if it shattered her heart and meant she didn't have a life with Joel, which was what she'd prayed for.

Suddenly, the diner door opened, and both women spun around to see who was there.

"It's only me," Wyatt called as he entered. "I've come to check that window."

Martha smiled. Joel was still looking out for her. No matter they could never be together.

"We have six passengers today," Martha said, as Wyatt moved toward the window, tools in his hand.

Wyatt turned to face her. "I will be back before they arrive. Don't worry." Martha had been worried. Beth was close to delivering her baby, and she was uncertain Wyatt would be there to ensure nothing went awry. "Besides, if anything happened, I know Joel would be happy to step in." He winked at her then, and Martha felt heat creep up her face.

When she glanced at Allie, the other woman was trying to hold back a smile. Martha's gaze went from Allie to Wyatt. He was openly grinning. Did no one have an inkling of sense? They both knew she and Joel had long parted.

They may have feelings for each other, but things had not worked out in that regard. Of course, that was because of the pressure Dennis and the other townsfolk had put on them both. As the self-proclaimed Crystal Springs matchmaker, he'd taken it upon himself to pair them up.

It wasn't as though there was no spark between them, as the opposite was true. Martha's heart fluttered at the thought of Joel. When he held her, warmth flooded her. When he kissed her, no one else existed.

"The window seems to be fixed now. If you have any further problems with it, or any of the others, let me know." Wyatt's words brought Martha back to her senses.

"I will," she said, wiping her hands on the once white apron. Martha turned back to the pastry she'd set aside while she worked on the stew—it would be ready for supper, but the soup would be ready in time for lunch.

Some days it was a juggling act to get everything ready in time, but Allie was a godsend. Martha was lucky to have her.

Allie opened the oven and spooned fat over the stuffed goose that was roasting there.

"I think I need to eat here tonight," Wyatt joked as he left the kitchen. Martha knew he wouldn't. He preferred to eat at home with his family, and why wouldn't he?

Her mind wandered to Joel once again, and she sighed. *Concentrate*, she scolded herself. Trouble was, with Joel's bakery so close by, she saw him daily. Some days, it was merely a glance. Other times, he purposely came out and talked to her.

She could walk to work via another route, but the truth was, she didn't want to. Martha's heart fluttered whenever she caught a glimpse of Joel, and his presence made her happy.

Why, then, did she continue to push him away? She would probably never know the answer.

Six passengers and two stage staff for meals tonight. Sometimes it was more, but with their regular supper service, there was no time limit. With the stage passengers, there was.

Lunch was their busiest time. Although the occasional business lunch was held there, it was mostly local women getting together with friends, or the ladies auxiliary. Many were close friends because of their affiliation with the church and their charity work.

Even in a town such as Crystal Springs, there were people in need. Not so much in the heart of town, although there were a handful. Martha knew of women who had become widows and left with small children. It was difficult for them with no income from their husbands. The ladies auxiliary prepared baskets of food each week for those in need. They visited the families and took toys for the children.

Where needed, clothes were provided for both mothers and children.

Those who could afford it donated to the church for this purpose. Whether that was goods or money didn't matter—every little bit helped.

When Beth was running the diner, she always prepared additional food for this purpose and ensured it was fresh when the ladies were doing their food run. Martha had continued that tradition. "These biscuits are for the food baskets," Martha told Allie as she finished packing them into a basket. "I won't have time to take them today, so it will be your task to deliver them."

As she glanced at Allie, she had the strangest feeling. The other woman's lips lifted slightly, as though she was holding back a smile. It made Martha wonder what she was planning. Knowing Allie, it could be anything.

Suddenly, the diner door opened. Was Wyatt back already? What had he forgotten? She shook herself mentally. He wasn't due for quite some time. If not Wyatt, then who?

"It's only me," a familiar voice called. "Thanks for this, Allie," Joel said a short time later, handing her a box of pastries. "I appreciate you taking them to the church with whatever you are taking."

Martha stared. Her gaze went from one to the other. At first, she believed the pair had concocted this plan to get her and Joel together. Then it occurred to her the plan was Allie's alone. Joel would never go along with such an underhanded scheme. Would he?

Her last thought got Martha thinking. Joel had made his feelings perfectly clear. He was determined to get them back together, and so was Allie. She opened her mouth, ready to make accusations, but thought the better of it. The Joel she knew would never do such a thing.

Even out of desperation.

"Yes, thanks, Allie," Martha said, her eyes piercing her friend. It was crystal clear what was going on. Allie was setting them up. If she pushed the two together, even in casual circumstances, the kitchen assistant thought it would get them back together.

If only it was as simple as that.

"I guess I should get back to the bakery," Joel said. He turned away without another word, and Martha's heart sank. He'd said barely a word to her, and it cut through her. Why was she fighting it? She truly did like Joel.

No, that was a lie. Martha loved Joel and had for a very long time. "Joel?" she said as he walked away from her.

He turned back to face her, a smile on his face. "What can I do for you?" he said, suddenly looking smug. Fury filled her, and Martha waved a hand in front of herself.

"Have a good day," she said between gritted teeth. It was now clear the two were in cahoots. Martha was having none of it.

Chapter Four

Joel couldn't contain his happiness until Martha's expression suddenly changed. She always could read him, and he'd let his guard down.

Next time he wanted to scheme to get close to her, he wouldn't involve Allie. Not only had Martha gotten mad at him, she would probably blame her assistant for her involvement. That wasn't fair. It was completely his decision to bring the pastries to the diner. In fact, although he knew Allie wanted to get them together again, she was against his scheming.

He should have listened. Apart from Beth, Allie knew Martha better than most people in town. He would have to be more mindful in the future. Instead of scheming and planning, he needed to be upfront. She had never liked liars or schemers. He should have never tried to be sneaky like this. Not that she was a vindictive person, but Martha may hold it against him.

He glanced from Martha to Allie. The younger woman had warned him. Martha was astute and could pick a lie a mile away. Joel didn't see it as a lie. Not really. Allie had offered to take his pastries to the auxiliary ladies, but not until he had suggested it.

"Alright," he burst out, almost forcefully. "It was my idea and my fault. Allie told me not to do it!"

"Not to do what?" she said sweetly, as though she hadn't guessed what he was up to.

Joel stared at her momentarily, then shrugged. "I'm sorry," he said gruffly, then strode away, closing the door behind him.

What had he done? Joel knew second chances didn't come along often, and now he'd blown it. He had totally messed up. Martha may never forgive him for doing such a stupid and reckless thing. Especially for trying his ruse to trick her.

All he wanted was an opportunity to get back together with the woman he loved. Was that too much to ask? He didn't think it was.

Arriving back at the bakery, Mrs. Cavendish stood outside, waiting. "Good morning, Mrs. Cavendish. Back so soon?" he asked. This was her second visit this week.

"I need some supplies, but I wondered if you would mind putting this notice in the window? My Molly is looking for work." She screwed up her face at the words, but handed the notice over, anyway. For his fussy customer, her daughter working somewhere menial, like a store, would be below her station, but Crystal Springs did not offer many opportunities.

Joel stared at the words. What had he been promising himself for months now? More time for himself. The only way he would achieve that was to appoint someone to help in the store.

He glanced up at Mrs. Cavendish. Did he really want to deal with the woman? She could be quite overwhelming at times. "I have an opening," he said without thinking. But it was too late to take the words back. Instead, he might as well forge ahead. "If Molly is suitable, I would consider putting her on trial to see if we're a good fit."

The woman's face lit up, then she suddenly snatched the notice she'd previously handed to him. "Molly will be so pleased," she said, as though her daughter's fate was sealed.

Joel groaned inwardly. "Send her along at ten tomorrow for an interview, and we'll go from there."

Suddenly Mrs. Cavendish looked uncomfortable. It was unlike the customer he saw regularly. "She's outside now. Window shopping. I could get her?" She turned toward the door, one hand pointing to the door, her body half turned. She was overly eager, and it worried Joel.

"Oh," he said, feigning interest, when in reality he was now concerned. He spotted Molly across the road. Why hadn't she brought the notice in herself? Joel was certain her mother was equally assertive with her family as she was with him. "If that suits Molly, I am free at this moment."

She didn't wait a moment longer. The door to the bakery was open before Joel could blink an eye. Mrs. Cavendish sprinted across the road so quickly it bothered Joel. She didn't check to see if anyone was coming, not even a wagon. Then again, she would surely hear if a wagon was hurtling toward her.

The memory of the wagon accident all those years ago forced itself into his mind. It was a terrible tragedy, one the townsfolk of Crystal Springs would not forget.

"Mr. Evans," his long-time customer said as she opened the bakery door again. "This is my daughter, Molly."

She stood back and allowed Molly to enter. It had been quite some time since he'd set eyes on Molly. She was a real beauty, but was she capable of managing a store? That was where his interest lay. "Pleased to meet you, Miss Cavendish," he said politely. "Please take a seat. I'm sure your mother doesn't mind leaving us alone for our interview. I'll close the store so we're not disturbed." He gazed at the older woman, who appeared quite agitated by his suggestion she leave. Molly was not a young girl. Had that been the case, it would be inappropriate. She was, however, at least twenty-five, perhaps a little older. Besides, the glass windows at the front of the bakery meant they could be clearly seen.

Joel was certain he heard the woman harrumph as she closed the door behind her. "Give me a moment," he said as he locked the door and turned the sign, telling customers he would be back soon.

He studied Molly as he sat down opposite her. She appeared nervous, but he guessed she was nowhere near as nervous as he was. In all the years he'd been a baker, he'd never hired help. More's the pity—his life had been consumed with his work for far too many years. "What experience do you have, Miss Cavendish?" he asked firmly, despite believing she'd had none.

She peered down at her hands as they sat on the table. "None," she whispered, her eyes flicking up momentarily as she spoke. She straightened her shoulders, as her mother had no doubt told her hundreds of times. "Call me Molly," she said moments later. Then she smiled. Her entire face lit up, and he knew his customers were going to like Molly Cavendish standing behind the counter instead of him.

"Would you like a coffee, Molly? I have tea if you'd prefer that?" He was not sure why he offered her a beverage. Joel had intended to make this interview short. Truth be told, it should be longer if he wanted someone capable.

"Tea would be nice, thank you." Suddenly she jumped up. "Perhaps if you show me where everything is kept, I could do the honors?"

She was keen, he would give her that. He wouldn't deny her the opportunity to show him what she could do. If his assumption was right, it would be very little. He imagined the Cavendishs had a slew of servants. Joel immediately admonished himself for his unfounded judgement. Who, around here, would have servants? "It's just through here," he said, pushing his own chair back. He felt the beady eyes of her mother on him and cursed the glass windows he'd installed a while back. Any other time, he enjoyed them. It meant he could see the comings and goings on the townsfolk, but especially Martha. It allowed him to rush outside when she got close.

Joel guided Molly into the kitchen. "This is bigger than I expected," she exclaimed, looking almost bewildered. "You keep it spotless. Would that be part of *my* job?" Suddenly, she appeared worried.

"That's my domain," he said. "You would work out the front, behind the counter. Few customers eat and drink here, but some do. The store itself would be your responsibility."

She nodded and watched as he showed her where everything was kept. Molly reached for two mugs and filled them. One with coffee, the other with tea. She then carried them out to the front of the store and placed them on the table.

Joel was impressed. He'd obviously jumped to conclusions about the family. Most likely because Mrs. Cavendish put on airs every time she entered his store. No matter, Molly seemed to differ totally from her mother. He waited for her to sit, then sat down opposite her again. "Thank you, Molly," he said. "You did well." She smiled, pleased with herself as she should be.

He lifted his mug and sipped the hot beverage. "It's delicious. Have you worked in a store before?" Her eyes averted again. "It's not a problem if you haven't. I can teach you."

She lifted her eyes again. "I'm a quick learner. You'll see." She looked horrified then. "If you give me the job, that is. I didn't mean to imply…" Molly frowned and looked ready to burst into tears.

Trying to prevent a difficult situation, Joel stood and went behind the counter, indicating for Molly to follow him. "This would be your domain," he said, spreading his hands to show the area she would work in. "I start work quite early. Usually around five at the latest."

"In the morning?" Shock settled on her face. It made Joel laugh.

"In the morning. Then I'm here the entire day until I close the store around three, depending on how busy it is." He watched as the color drained from her face. "You understand *you* won't need to start work at that early hour, don't you?"

He saw the relief cross her face. "Thank goodness," she said, almost laughing.

"That's the time I begin baking for the day. I open the store as soon as the baked goods are cool enough to sell. Sometimes earlier," he said, recalling the number of times he'd had to open for Wyatt. "Would eight work for you?"

Molly smiled with relief. "It would. Do you mind?" she asked, opening drawers and looking into cabinets behind the counter.

Joel grinned. "Not at all." So far, the interview had gone well. He showed Molly where the till was kept and showed her how he showcased items he wanted to push. She was attentive and seemed to be a quick learner, as she'd already indicated.

She seemed far more relaxed now, but didn't say another word. It was as if she was waiting for him to say something. Of course. What a fool he was.

"Now you've had the grand tour, and understand how the bakery works, would you be prepared to undertake a trial period of, say, two weeks? Starting tomorrow. Only if that's suitable, of course."

Molly's smile lit up her face. "That sounds lovely. Thank you, Mr. Evans."

"Joel," he said, shaking her hand. "I'll see you at eight tomorrow. Tell your mother to tear up that sign, will you?"

He noticed a skip in Molly's step as she left the bakery. His life would be far easier from now on. At least he hoped it would. How he would tell Martha he did not know, but he wasn't certain his new assistant would make her particularly happy.

Chapter Five

Martha braced herself. Any moment now, the stagecoach would arrive. That meant it wouldn't be long before they had a bevy of customers in the diner. She glanced across the tables and nodded. Allie had double checked all the tables were set correctly, and the chairs were all in place.

In the kitchen, everything was as it should be. The stuffed goose was cooked to perfection, and the last of the desserts were about to come out of the oven. The kettle was boiling, and mugs were at the ready. Martha took a long fortifying breath, then let it out slowly—as she did before each supper service. She was fully aware of how hectic things were about to become.

Right on time, Wyatt strode through the diner door. "Evening ladies," he said cheerfully, as he always did. "Are we ready for the onslaught?"

Martha rolled her eyes. He asked the same question practically every week. "Maybe," she said teasingly. Wyatt's eyebrows rose. "Of course we are," she said as she laughed. "We are well organized, as always."

Moments later, the door to the diner opened again. "Evening, Connor," Wyatt said to the stage driver. Connor was one of many drivers they saw in the diner.

"Evening, Sheriff," Connor said as he winked. He knew very well Wyatt had not been the sheriff of Crystal Springs for a good two years, yet continued to call him such.

Wyatt was used to it, and laughed. "Take a seat," he told the other man.

It wasn't long before the passengers all pushed their way into the diner. "Easy," Wyatt told them. "There's plenty of room, and plenty of food. No one will miss out."

She watched as one particular cowboy strutted in, seemingly full of his own importance. It didn't sit well with Martha. Immediately, she had a dislike for the man. Perhaps it was unfounded, but felt certain it wasn't.

She followed Wyatt's gaze and saw it was trained on the cowboy. He appeared far from happy.

Allie came forward and guided their guests to their seats, then read the menu to them. "Our special of the day is roasted goose with stuffing and vegetables," she began, "and for those who prefer a lighter meal, hearty beef stew."

Allie poured water from the jug into individual glasses, and had almost finished. Martha was about to turn back to the kitchen when she heard an almighty yelp. "Ow!" Allie yelled. "How dare you!"

Wyatt was by Allie's side in moments. "Cowboy," he said firmly. "Don't touch the ladies or you'll be out on your behind so fast you won't know what hit you." He stared the cowboy down to the degree the man, who was a good match for Wyatt size-wise, cringed. "Now apologize to the lady."

"Yessir," the cowboy said without hesitation. "Ma'am, I apologize profusely. Won't happen again."

He appeared far from sorry, and Martha knew Wyatt would keep a special eye on this particular customer. "Cowboy," Wyatt said firmly, "you just earned yourself the ugliest waitress in the joint. Now keep your grubby hands to yourself." He turned to Allie. "You alright?"

"I'm fine, thank you, Wyatt," she said with a shaky voice, then turned toward the kitchen. Martha could see she wasn't fine. Far from it. Moments later, she heard the diner door open.

Martha glanced up to see Joel standing there. He hurried toward Wyatt, and the two men murmured, their voices so low they couldn't be heard in the kitchen. "I'll take the orders," Martha told Allie. "You stay here and start dishing up—two of each meal to begin with. I'll find out what is needed."

Entering the dining room, she glanced Joel's way. Warmth filled her. How could she feel this way just from seeing the man? He smiled tentatively, and she knew Wyatt had told him what had happened. The two men had their gazes trained on the vile cowboy who had changed everything.

"Who's having what?" Martha asked, her good manners seemingly lost to her momentarily. Her fury was getting the better of her, and she felt Joel's gaze on her. He moved toward her and stayed less than a step behind. He was as protective as ever, and it felt good.

None of the passengers said a word. She rolled her eyes. The entire night was going to be tiresome, she could feel it. "Put your hand up if you want the goose?" Five hands went up. Without another word, she spun around and returned to the kitchen. "Five for the goose," she told Allie, then studied the younger woman. "You stay in the kitchen tonight. Not that I expect that fool to try anything again. Joel's here too."

For the first time since she arrived back in the kitchen, Allie turned to face her. She was smiling, which was a good sign. "He couldn't keep away," Allie said, and chuckled.

Martha couldn't help but roll her eyes again. "He was walking past and saw the ruckus," she said, then carried the first two meals out to the dining room. "You keep dishing up. I'll be back shortly."

The rest of the evening went smoothly, and without incident. When their guests were all gone, Joel turned to leave. "I'll catch you all later," he said when the diner was quiet again. "Unless there's something I can do to help?"

Wyatt's gaze went first to Joel, and then Martha. "I appreciate your help tonight. Have you eaten? There's usually plenty left."

"I wouldn't want to be a bother," Joel said firmly. "Besides, I didn't do much."

Allie interrupted. "Your presence, both of you, made me feel much more at ease." She screwed up her face as if remembering the cowboy's hands on her.

Martha put an arm around her friend. "It won't happen again. I won't let it," she said.

"We won't let it happen again," Joel said decisively. "Why any man would think that's alright, I don't know. I'll be here each night to ensure it doesn't occur again."

"Thank you, but there's no need," Martha told him. "Besides, Wyatt is here when the stage comes through."

"I'm not talking about once a week. I mean, every night. It could happen any time." He rubbed a hand across his beard. "I'm sorry I didn't realize the danger you ladies were in."

He glanced across at Wyatt. A shudder went through Martha. Were they really in danger? Had Beth had to contend with rowdy cowboys in her time? The thought sent cold shivers down her spine.

Joel stepped closer. His arm went up around her, and he pulled her close. She didn't shrug him away, although Martha knew she should. "It must have been awful for you," he told Allie. "I promise you, both of you, it won't happen again."

Martha nodded. She knew Joel would be true to his word.

"The meal was delicious," Joel announced. "I still maintain you didn't need to do it."

Martha tried to hold back a smile, but couldn't. It had been a very long time since she'd shared a meal with Joel. Despite Allie being there with them, their time together seemed rather intimate. Special. She'd missed those times they'd spent together before they agreed to part.

It took a moment before she remembered why they'd split. It was the pressure. When the town matchmaker declares you should be together, you try to prove him wrong. Besides, Dennis wasn't married, so who made him the expert?

"I need to tell you something," Joel said between mouthfuls of coffee. He stared at her, and Martha suddenly felt uncomfortable.

"I'll leave you two alone," Allie said, and pushed back her chair.

Joel turned his gaze on Allie, a frown on his face. "No, stay. It's nothing personal." He waited for Allie to seat herself again, then took another mouthful of coffee. "I've hired someone to help in the bakery."

Martha hadn't realized she was holding her breath, and it came out in a rush. "Finally," she said. "How long have you been saying you need help?"

"Far too long. I've hired Molly Cavendish. She seems capable." Joel's expression almost begged her to agree. It wasn't her place to say one way or the other.

"I truly hope it helps. You work far too hard and always have." Martha knew Molly. She was beautiful, but she was far younger than either of them. But with Molly right under his nose, would Joel look to greener pastures? She shook the thought aside. Joel had told her time after time he had eyes only for her. His heart was hers, she knew it was, but would he give up and look elsewhere?

Martha sighed. She loved Joel far more than she would ever admit. They'd had their chance, and that was the end of it.

"I didn't want you to be shocked when you saw her at the counter in the morning," he said. "Speaking of morning, I should go. But first I'll escort you ladies home. I'll do that every night from now on."

Martha studied him. Did he not know their routine? "Wyatt accompanies both of us home each night after the supper service is over."

Joel grinned. "I'm taking over from him. Beth is almost ready to deliver their baby, so it makes sense. Besides, it will take the pressure off him and give him more time with his family. I'll let him know tomorrow."

"You need to get to sleep early. Your days start with the birds." Martha couldn't help but protest—she was worried about Joel's health.

He frowned momentarily, then smiled. "Thank you for your concern, Martha, but I promise I'll be fine." He stood then and lifted his soiled plates. Martha put her hand over his to stop him and immediately regretted it. A zing ran through her, and it jolted her. Joel's head snapped up, proving he felt it too.

"I… I can do that," she said, her voice shaky. Why was she so shaken? She'd encountered it before. When they were together.

He didn't say a word, only nodded. When she glanced across at Allie, she was smiling. As irritated as she felt, Martha didn't say another word. She gathered up the soiled dishes and headed to the kitchen.

Joel followed her there. As she poured boiling water over the dishes, he was right behind her. As she washed, he dried. Not a word was exchanged. She felt strangely comforted by his presence. Martha knew she shouldn't, but felt elated.

Joel had insinuated himself back into her life, and she wasn't complaining.

Chapter Six

It seemed strange to not be rushing about in the bakery. She had only been here a few hours, but already Molly was making a difference.

Joel could spend more time in the kitchen baking and cleaning, and less time on the front counter. As much as he enjoyed the interaction with customers, he now realized how much of a toll doing everything was taking on him.

He carried a tray of freshly baked pastries out to the store. Molly stood behind the counter, waiting for the next customers to arrive. "I can do that for you," she said, as he bent to add them to the display cabinet.

Joel was truly grateful for having hired Molly. So far anyway. What transpired over the next two weeks would be the true gauge of the future.

He headed back into his domain, the place where he felt most comfortable—his kitchen. Since he didn't have to set out the pastries in the cabinet, he got straight into cleaning. He was pedantic when it came to cleanliness. It was one of the many ways he and Martha were like-minded. They both ensured their workspace was spotless, and wouldn't have it any other way.

He'd noticed Molly was keeping her workspace clean as well. It was an immense relief to him. There might even come a time when he felt comfortable enough to leave her alone in the store. For short bursts at first, then perhaps longer.

But he was getting ahead of himself. At least for the next week, he would be here to supervise Molly. The bakery was unfamiliar territory for her, and the last thing he wanted was to see her floundering. If she felt out of her depth, Molly was likely to leave before her trial time was even over. That wouldn't do.

Joel plunged the cloth into hot, soapy water. It was so hot, he almost burned himself, but it was how he liked it. Hot water killed the germs. Cold water did not.

Not that germs had a chance in his kitchen. He scrubbed the countertop, then the island bench he used to make bread. The larger surface was more conducive to kneading the bread. He wondered if Martha was making bread right now. Or maybe she was baking biscuits. Whatever she was doing, Joel wished he were with her.

Perhaps he could find a reason to visit the diner? He'd think about that for a few minutes while he finished cleaning his kitchen.

His thoughts were interrupted when Molly returned the pastry tray. "All done," she said. "Is there anything else you would like me to do?"

She was eager. He'd give her that. So far, so good. "Make sure there are enough paper bags for pastries and enough paper to wrap the bread. Those always need to be well stocked."

Molly fiddled with her apron. "Of course," she said rather flippantly. Had he made her sound like a fool? It wasn't his intention.

"I didn't mean…" He studied her. Did Molly seem upset? Joel didn't know her well enough to tell. "Ask if there's anything you need help with or don't understand. Starting a new job can be overwhelming."

She nodded, then hurried away.

Molly had no sooner gone than he heard the tinkle of the bell over the door. Low murmurings wafted into the bakery kitchen. He wanted to see who was there, but used his willpower to stop himself from butting in. It wouldn't be fair to Molly.

Moments later, Molly entered the kitchen. "Sheriff Holt is here and wants to talk to you." The moment she'd passed on the message, Molly went back to her station.

He wanted to tell her Wyatt was no longer sheriff, but didn't get the chance. No matter, he would tell her later.

Joel brushed the flour off his apron and went out to the store. "Is everything alright, Wyatt? Is Martha…"

Wyatt grinned. "Martha is fine, but Beth is in labor. I need to ensure you can man the diner tonight, and get the ladies home safely."

Joel was certain Wyatt knew he would, but needed to confirm for himself. "I will, I promise. Don't worry about either woman. Beth is your only concern." He could feel Molly's gaze on him, but didn't believe there was any animosity. She wouldn't know many of the townsfolk, as her mother kept her fairly isolated. It was a miracle she'd been allowed to go out to work.

Wyatt reached out a hand to his best friend. "I can't thank you enough."

Joel leaned in and turned the handshake into a hug. "Looking after that wife of yours is all the thanks needed." Joel knew he sounded emotional, but he couldn't help it. He and Wyatt had been friends since the other man had arrived in town. They were now closer than ever. It filled his heart with joy to see his friend happy. "Wait," he said as Wyatt retreated. "A pastry for that boy of yours. He needs to be spoiled today."

"Elijah would want me to say thank you on his behalf."

Joel handed him a pastry in a paper bag and Wyatt left without another word.

Locking up the store, Joel felt more relaxed than he had for a very long time. Having Molly working at the store had already made a tremendous difference, and it was only day one of her trial. Unless there was a massive problem in the future, he saw no reason to not keep her on.

It meant he would lose money by paying her, but it also meant more time for baking. On an average day, he ran out of baked goods well before the store closed. Simply because he couldn't do everything.

He'd been thinking about adding to his repertoire. There was so much he could add to his bakery and needed to think about it further. The bakery and diner had never competed, and he had no intention of starting now. That meant apple pie and cherry cobbler was out. Besides, they were better eaten hot.

Fruit cake flashed into his mind, along with a variety of slices, muffins, and cupcakes.

Joel shook himself mentally. One day was not long enough to gauge the long term. Still, it surely couldn't hurt to dream?

He headed toward the diner. It was a little early, but it wasn't worthwhile going home. He knew Martha would have coffee at the ready, and he would indulge. Normally at this time of day, he refrained, but filling in time meant he would change his normal routine.

As he opened the diner door, it dawned on Joel this would be his new normal. He'd promised to assist the ladies every evening, and that's exactly what he planned to do. It wasn't like it was a hardship—it was a blessing in disguise. Not only would he be there to protect Allie and Martha, he'd get to spend more time with the love of his life. "Martha?" Joel called as he entered. Both he and Wyatt had tried to get the women to lock the door when the diner wasn't open. Anyone could enter, and if they were quiet enough, no one would know until it was too late. He turned the latch, so at least for now they were more protected.

It wasn't long before Martha stood in the kitchen's doorway, her once pristine apron covered in all manner of food. He knew first-hand how messy it could get in a commercial kitchen, having experienced it on a daily basis.

The closer he was to the kitchen, the clearer her face. She smiled, but didn't say a word. When they were only inches apart, he stared into her big blue eyes. He reached out and brushed back a tendril of hair that had worked its way loose. His eyes didn't leave hers for even a moment.

If Allie hadn't been there, Joel knew he would have leaned in and kissed Martha. With Allie there, he knew Martha would object. "Beth is in labor," he said, and heard a squeal from within the kitchen. Allie suddenly appeared, a massive smile on her face.

"I hope it's going well," Martha said, her smile growing bigger. "When did you find out?"

It was time to confess. "Wyatt called in a few hours ago to ensure I would be here tonight."

The smiles disappeared. "A few hours ago?"

"I…" Joel frowned. Perhaps he could have told them sooner. Especially with Molly at the bakery. "I'm sorry. I didn't think it would make any difference." He shrugged his shoulders. It really didn't make a difference, but he could have told them earlier. The truth couldn't be denied. "Molly seems to be working out," he said, trying to change the subject to something more palatable. To himself, anyway.

Martha nodded tersely and turned away. "I have to get this finished," she called over her shoulder. Before he had a chance to say anything more, Allie was next to him, holding a mug of coffee. He breathed in the aroma.

The diner had a reputation for the best coffee in town. He sold coffee at the bakery, but most people preferred the diner's brew. Joel didn't blame them—it was far superior. He wondered if Molly's coffee would entice more customers to go to the bakery? She was also far better to look at than he was.

"What can I do to help?" he asked no one in particular.

Allie continued to stand in front of him. "Go to the dining room and sit down." He shrugged his shoulders again and did as he was told. He took that as meaning he was in the way. The moment he sat, Allie placed the coffee on the table in front of him, along with a plate with two muffins—one lemon, and one blueberry, his favorite.

"You didn't have to," he said, but she smiled and turned away.

"Let me know if you need more," she called over her shoulder. Joel sipped the coffee. As always, it was perfect. He wasn't sure what those ladies did to make their coffee so good, but he liked it. Maybe it was the fact it was freshly brewed? His coffee could sit there for hours before anyone purchased it. His mind went back to the previous day when Molly made his coffee. It was far better than any he'd made, and she'd made it fresh in front of him.

Joel didn't think he was a slower learner, but this was certainly a lesson he wouldn't forget. From now on, coffee would be freshly made as it was ordered. He would even make a sign to that effect. That surely didn't count as competing with the diner? He shook his head. He was certain it didn't.

He glanced down at the muffins sitting on the plate in front of him. Joel had always loved Martha's cooking. He'd even tried to get her to work for him, but she wasn't interested. Bread and pastries didn't interest her one iota, she told him every time he asked. Finally, he gave up asking.

Her interest lay in cooking meals, rather than baking. Not that she minded creating desserts—she enjoyed that too. In fact, he was almost certain that was her favorite part of the job. She liked to come up with a variety of desserts as well.

Wyatt and Beth gave her free rein of the diner. It seemed to Joel she should simply buy the diner. Then again, as an employee, she didn't have the worry of ensuring costs were covered, or making repairs, and the other million things that went to running a business. He could see why she would stick to the thing she loved best—cooking.

He took a mouthful of the lemon muffin. It was still warm—just the way he liked them. His mouth tingled from the flavor bursting in there. He'd almost forgotten how good Martha's muffins were. They were far better than his. There was no denying it.

"Everything alright out here?" Allie asked.

"Mmmm," Joel mumbled, his mouth full of lemon muffin. He couldn't wait to start on the blueberry muffin. These would certainly tide him over until supper. "Delicious," he said when his mouth was finally empty. "You ladies spoil me."

Allie smiled, almost conspiratorially. What was she up to? "Do we?" she asked, a cheeky grin on her face. She then turned and trotted back into the kitchen.

It wouldn't be long before the supper service began. Joel needed to prepare. It wasn't like there would be an onslaught of customers, but he vowed to protect both women, and that's exactly what he would do.

If that helped get Martha endeared to him in the process, so be it.

Chapter Seven

Once the doors to the diner opened, customers usually filed in slowly and with dignity. Tonight was different.

It was Saturday night, and the cowboys from outlying ranches had been paid. First, they would have a decent meal, then they would frequent the saloon. The fact they were sober when they arrived was a plus.

"Evening, everyone," Joel said as they stormed into the diner. "Slow and steady does it. There is plenty for everyone." Allie stood at the doorway to the kitchen, and all heads turned her way. Wolf whistles rang out across the diner. "First rule." Joel shouted above the ruckus to make himself heard. "Do not touch the ladies. Break that rule and I'll turf you out. You will never be allowed back."

Martha watched the color drain from the faces of a few of the cowboys. They all knew there were no other decent eating places in town. The saloon food was barely edible. The noise died down and Allie approached him. Her experience with another cowboy had left her nervous, which was not surprising.

"Welcome everyone," Allie said, her voice louder than usual. Martha watched as Joel edged closer to Allie, ensuring she was near to him. "Tonight's menu comprises roast lamb and roasted chicken." Most of the ranches were beef ranches, so they knew better than to serve beef on a Saturday night. "Dessert is a choice of cherry cobbler, and raspberry summer pudding."

So far, so good. Wyatt was firm, and everyone who'd been in Crystal Springs knew he had been the town's sheriff and wouldn't let them get away with anything. Would Joel be able to keep them in hand, or would they endeavor to test him? He was a big man, every bit as big as Wyatt, so she hoped that would be enough to keep the cowboys in hand.

Joel stepped forward. "Raise your hand if you want roast lamb." A sea of hands went up, and Allie wrote the numbers. "Roasted chicken?" The remaining hands were raised.

"Thank you, Joel," Allie said as she turned toward the kitchen.

Martha nodded his way and smiled. She would have taken Allie's place in a heartbeat, but Allie refused the offer. They both knew she had a job to do and needed to get out there. So far, so good. Their rowdy customers had settled right down once Joel had taken charge of the dining room. Martha was grateful for Joel's presence, even if she had refused it to begin with. Right now, she understood how truly stupid that was. She went into the kitchen with Allie and began plating up the meals. Luckily, she was used to Saturday nights and the large number of cowboys who wanted a good home-cooked meal each week.

The majority were well behaved, but a few still had to learn to keep their hands to themselves. Mostly the younger ones, but Wyatt always kept a close watch on them, and Joel was no different.

The two women carried three plates of food each to the tables, served the first round of meals, then hurried back to collect more. They repeated the process until everyone had been served.

Suddenly, the noise level was high. Men eating and talking at the same time. Martha thanked her lucky stars she and Allie were in another room. Poor Joel. He wasn't used to the cacophony that resulted. She peeked out the kitchen door and noticed he was frowning. Should she go to him?

He had positioned himself at the front counter, which was close to the entrance. Wyatt always stayed there, too. Not only was there a tall stool to sit on, he could block anyone from leaving who hadn't paid for their meal.

"This is for you," Martha said, handing him a mug of coffee. "When everyone is gone, we'll have a quiet supper."

Joel's face screwed up. "They are a noisy lot."

Martha couldn't help but laugh. "Sometimes the noise level is even worse than this."

Now he appeared shocked. "Worse than this? How do you tolerate it?"

She studied him for a long moment. "It's my job. Besides, you don't even notice after a while." It was true. The first few times, the noise gave her a headache. After that, she was too busy to worry. Wyatt had kept the noise low, but it had been an effort. He'd given up after a while—she'd agreed it wasn't worth it when it was an impossible task.

Martha glanced about. Most of the men had finished eating. She moved closer to collect their soiled plates. "Don't even think about it, Clancy," she said, noticing the young cowboy lift his hand. "See that man over there?" She indicated Joel. "He's my betrothed." Joel's head snapped up. She hadn't meant for him to hear. Martha had merely tried to scare the young man off. It worked; his hand went down quickly.

Laughter surrounded her. Martha wasn't sure if they were laughing at Clancy, or whether they were laughing because they didn't believe her. Martha dropped the plates back on the table and strode toward Joel. His gaze pierced her, but she continued on her trek.

Stepping behind the counter, she leaned in and kissed him—right on the lips. Martha heard Joel gasp, then his arms came up around her. Whistling surrounded them. Suddenly, she pulled away. There were soiled dishes to be collected and washed. When she stared into Joel's face, he was grinning.

He looked far happier than she'd seen him for a very long time.

With the diner closed and the cowboys gone, they finally had time to sit down and eat. There wasn't a lot left, but enough to feed the three of them. "You did great, Joel," Martha told him. "I'm sorry I kissed you earlier."

Allie's head snapped up. "You did what? Good for you!"

Joel grinned. "I didn't push her away, either." His grin widened. "Will you do that every night?"

Martha glared at him. "Highly unlikely. I only did it to put Clancy in his place. Notice he didn't try anything after that."

"Clancy is sweet," Allie said. "He wouldn't hurt a fly." Joel watched the conversation between her and

Allie. He didn't know the cowboys, Martha was certain. They only came to town once a week, and he was usually home by then.

Joel suddenly spoke up. "Are you certain about that, Allie? You can't be too careful these days."

Allie floundered. "I… maybe, I'm not sure. I've never seen him away from the diner."

"No matter, I'll walk you both home. Better safe than sorry." He drank down the last mouthful of his coffee.

"I wonder how Beth is doing," Martha said. "I hope everything is going well."

Joel frowned at her. "Wyatt would have let us know if there was a problem. Wouldn't he?" Quiet descended over them. "Maybe I should go there and find out."

"Not without me," Martha said firmly.

Allie spoke up too. "Or me."

They quickly cleaned up between the three of them and headed toward Wyatt and Beth's house. Walking along the normally quiet streets, they could hear the noise from the saloon. Crystal Springs was once quiet. Why the mayor had allowed a saloon, she would never understand. His argument was it would bring revenue to the town.

Unfortunately, along with that came unsavory characters.

Martha moved closer to Joel. She might have been overreacting, but she was glad he was there. She'd certainly felt far safer walking home since Wyatt began escorting her and Allie. It might be one of the safest towns in Montana, but they still had the odd problem, mostly from visitors, but also from drunk locals at the saloon.

The cottage was lit up, and Martha could see movement inside. Wyatt stood in the sitting room, his back to the window. Elijah, Beth and Wyatt's young son, stood on a chair and was staring at his father, his eyes wide in astonishment. Did that mean…?

She knocked on the door. Not too loud that it would disturb Beth, but loud enough that Wyatt would hear. He slowly turned to face the front door. As he did so, she saw the small babe in his arms. There was a smile on his face, and relief washed over her. Wyatt would not be smiling if anything had happened to Beth. Her beautiful friend, Beth.

Tears filled Martha's eyes, even before the door opened. She wasn't sure if it was from happiness or relief, or even a mix of both. Joel turned to face her, and a hand went to her back. He pulled her close against his side. "It will be alright," he whispered.

She nodded. "Wyatt has a babe in his arms," she whispered back. Moments later, the door opened, and Martha was a sobbing mess. She felt so joyous for her friends and wanted to tell the world. For now, she would keep her voice low, ensuring she didn't scare the baby.

"It's a girl," Wyatt said, his voice full of pride. He stepped back and ushered them all in. "Do you want to hold her?" he asked Martha, and she nodded, afraid if she spoke she would start sobbing again.

The proud father handed over his daughter. "Beth is fine, but resting," he said. "Doc Ryan is still in there with her. Once he's gone, you can visit."

"What is her name?" Martha asked quietly.

"We decided on Rose, after Beth's mother." He smiled then. "Never did I believe I'd become a father. I was certain I'd left my run too late. And now," Wyatt said, his voice full of emotion, "I have two beautiful children. Only now do I understand God has been looking over my shoulder all my life, finding the right person to be my soulmate." He brushed at his eyes. Not that Wyatt would want anyone to think he was crying. Martha knew him better than that.

Martha sat on a chair with the baby still in her arms. "Sweet Rose," she said, then kissed Rose's forehead. "What do you think of your baby sister,

Elijah?" she asked the young boy, who seemed in shock.

He shrugged his little shoulders, his eyes still wide with astonishment.

Suddenly, the bedroom door opened and Doc Ryan strolled out. "Only one visitor at a time," he demanded. "Beth needs to rest."

"Of course," Wyatt said. "Are you ready to see your mama, Elijah?" Martha's godson spun around and headed toward the bedroom. "Quietly and slowly," Wyatt told him quietly. "Mama is very tired."

Elijah pouted. "Alright, Papa."

Warmth filled Martha. She wanted this for herself one day, but for now, this entire scenario filled her with joy. She pulled the new baby close to her chest. "Beautiful child of God," she whispered, and tears sprang to her eyes again.

"She certainly is," Joel said. "One day, *we* might have one of our own."

Martha's head shot up. She was ready to admonish Joel for his words, but knew she would not be unhappy about having Joel's babies. There were a lot of fences to mend before they could contemplate babies. Relinquishing their relationship because of interference from Dennis was a heartache she hadn't wanted. She wasn't sure if she was prepared to go through that all over again. The question was, could they forgive each other for bowing to the pressure Dennis had put on them? Then there was the question of whether or not they wanted to get married.

She wasn't sure if the thought of getting back with Joel thrilled her, or filled her with dread. Martha knew she couldn't bear falling for him all over again, only to endure heartache if it didn't work out.

Chapter Eight

Joel could have kicked himself.

The words were out of his mouth before he thought about what he was saying. Both he and Martha were past their prime, but their best friends had proven they could still have a family at a later age. He had pined for Martha for years.

Before he knew it, she was being courted and, in the blink of an eye, married. It had shattered him.

If her husband hadn't died from a heart attack, she would still be happily married right now.

Of course, it was his own fault—not once did he tell Martha how he felt.

He'd been stupid once and let her get away. Never again.

Joel's thoughts halted momentarily. Not only had he let her get away once, but twice. If Dennis hadn't interfered and tried to constantly push them together, would they be happily married now? Fury filled him. Dennis called himself a matchmaker, but his interference had torn the pair apart.

Unfortunately, he had little choice but to deal with Dennis for business purposes, otherwise the man would be banished from his life.

Perhaps he should make Dennis as miserable as he'd made him and Martha? Joel shook himself mentally. He would never do such a thing—it wasn't in him to be cruel or unpleasant to anyone. Not even someone he considered to be verging on being an enemy.

Joel's attention was pulled toward the bedroom. "You can go in now, Martha. I know Beth wants to see you." Wyatt reached out his arms for baby Rose. "Would you like to hold her, Allie?"

Martha stood. With baby Rose in her arms, she seemed a natural mother. If things didn't progress with the two of them soon, it could be too late. Martha was only a few years from forty, and he was now a touch over that dreaded age. It meant they were both fighting for time. Rose could be the catalyst to their relationship moving forward.

Allie eagerly took the little cherub. Her smile didn't waiver. She was far younger than any of them in the house right now, but he could see she longed for a baby. Is that what happened to Martha? The reason for the tears? He would probably never know, but he wanted her to be happy. And if that meant giving her a child, then so be it.

He just needed to convince her, albeit gently, they needed to be together for all eternity.

After dropping Allie off at her cottage, they headed toward Martha's home. It was close to Beth and Wyatt's place, and he could have taken Martha home first. He knew it was selfish, but Joel wanted to spend more time with her, not less, so he insisted she come along to take Allie home first.

"What a day!" Martha exclaimed when they were almost at her cottage. "Thank you for being there when I needed you."

Joel wasn't sure if she meant when she became emotional, or when the diner was filled with cowboys. Or, perhaps wishful thinking on his part, it could even be when she kissed him. Deep in his heart, he knew it was when they visited Beth and Wyatt. She likely wouldn't have gone there alone. Not this late at night, and not in the dark. Especially not with a bunch of drunken cowboys running around town.

He reached out and took her hand. "I'm always happy to help. I'm sure you know that." Moonlight shrouded her face, and Joel couldn't help but stare. Her eyes sparkled in the light of the full moon. Suddenly, she turned away and unlocked the door. His hand covered hers as she struggled. She was shaking, and it made him wonder why. Was it because of her elation over the new babe, or was she afraid of being alone with him?

Joel knew Martha wasn't afraid of him harming her. But he also knew she had feelings for him. Those feelings seemed to get stronger by the day. It surely wasn't a bad thing. "Martha," he said, then leaned closer as she turned to face him. "You must know how I feel about you?"

Without thinking, his hands were cupping her face. Her eyes sparkled and danced. They seemed to dare him to go further, to kiss her. And that's exactly what he did.

Martha stood rigid. But only for a matter of seconds. After that, she relaxed into him. Her arms slid up around his neck as she pulled him down to her level. Her lips were soft and pliable, and he didn't want the kiss to stop.

He remembered how it had been between them before. It was like this, only better. He'd been on the verge of asking her if she would marry him when Dennis interfered. The man was the devil incarnate, Joel was certain of it.

For now, he didn't want to think about Dennis. He only wanted to continue to kiss Martha, the love of his life.

Suddenly, her arms dropped from around his neck. She pulled back slightly and gazed up at him.

"We… we really shouldn't," she whispered into the darkness.

He glanced down at the sweet woman he still held in his arms. Joel never wanted to let her go, but knew there was no choice. Her head rested against his chest, and he desperately wanted to be with her. He would marry Martha in a heartbeat, but knew she wasn't ready.

"You're right," he said, unsure whether he should drop his arms from around her. He didn't want to do that—it felt good holding her like this. "I'll wait until you are inside. Lock the door the moment you are, and then I'll leave."

She stared up at him, disbelief all over her face. Had her words been a façade? Was she toying with him? Trying to entice him further. It was all Joel could do not to grin. He was certain he knew Martha well. Perhaps he didn't know her quite as much as he thought.

He would play along. Martha was the love of his life. His soulmate. If he had to pretend to not be interested, so be it.

Martha stepped back, her arms sliding away. He felt completely bereft and wanted to pull her back to him, but resisted the urge. He watched as she went inside. The latch clicked, and he turned away, heading toward his own home.

If it was games Martha wanted, he was ready to play. His heart was more than ready for a life with Martha Cooley.

Joel whistled all the way home. The words rolling around in his mind were simple—let the games begin!

Sunday was a favorite day for Joel.

Not only did he get to sleep in, he went to church. Stepping inside the church building was all it took to make him feel as though his soul had been refreshed. A warmth would come over him, and he felt… different. As though he was a better person because of it.

When Preacher Clyde Walters delivered his sermon, more often than not, the words spoke to his heart and his soul. He always left feeling fulfilled.

He drank down the last of his coffee—the coffee that didn't come close to the quality of the diner's coffee, but would have to do. He thought the secret was making it fresh, but this coffee was made only minutes ago. Did they use a different coffee than what Joel purchased? Perhaps Dennis was purchasing a unique type of coffee for the diner.

Once again, Dennis went down in his estimation.

Joel shook himself mentally. He had to stop obsessing about Dennis and start thinking more positively about himself and Martha being together. There was no way he could openly state he wanted to court her. She would run a mile.

He carried his soiled dishes to the sink and placed them in the soapy water. The temperature would be too hot to touch right now as he'd emptied the kettle into it. He would tend to that chore later. For now, he needed to get ready for church.

First, he would polish his boots. It was a task he undertook every Sunday morning without fail. Then he would trim his beard and wash. Cleanliness was next to godliness. Isn't that what they said?

After that, he would dress in his crisp white shirt, the tie he kept especially for church, and his suit. As a baker, he only needed one suit. There was no point spending money on something that was unnecessary.

They were all laid out on the bed, along with his best socks. Every Sunday, he went through the same ritual. Joel was a man of habit.

If he was lucky, he would get to sit near Martha. Or perhaps he should keep away from her today? She wanted to play games, and he could do that too.

Soon he was on his way to church. With a spring in his step, Joel whistled all the way to the Sunday service. He couldn't wait to get there.

Chapter Nine

Entering the church, Martha glanced about for Joel. She couldn't see him. It wasn't like Joel to miss the Sunday service. He was a stickler for arriving early, and usually found a place near to Wyatt and Beth, as well as her.

Wyatt had already sat down, along with Elijah. His son was fidgety today, and Martha could understand why. With a new baby in the house, he would be on edge. Not to mention his mother wasn't there—she usually was. Beth would be bed bound for at least the next few weeks, so Martha would ensure she did whatever she could to help.

God knew the family had looked out for her in the past. Not that it made a difference to Martha—she would always do what was right by anyone who needed her help.

"Good morning, Preacher Walters."

Martha's head turned as she heard Joel's voice at the back of the room. He was shaking the preacher's hand. As though he sensed her watching him, Joel's head shot up. Then he smiled tentatively and took his seat—at the very back of the church. She studied him as he opened his Bible and read from it. Then he closed his eyes and silently prayed.

She longed to be sitting beside him. They'd always sat together, Joel, Wyatt, Beth, and Martha. Even when little Elijah had arrived on the scene, they still stuck together. They were all friends. Always had been.

Her heart thudded. Was Joel distancing himself from her? Her heart shattered. The pain in her chest was unbearable. Martha would never recover if Joel shunned her—that wasn't what she wanted. But what did she want? She really wasn't sure, but knew a life without Joel in it was unconscionable.

The preacher ambled down the aisle toward the pulpit. The organ music seemed to drift into the background. Martha breathed deeply. It felt like there was no air in the room. She had to get outside. Except she was in church, God's place, and she couldn't make a scene.

She stood and ran. There was no choice. She needed air.

Faces stared at her as she went—they were all a blur. The only face that wasn't a haze was Joel's. He stared at her momentarily, then was out of his seat and right behind her. She didn't stop until she was outside in the fresh air. She took deep breaths.

Long and steady breaths of air. That's what she needed.

Tears filled her eyes out of fear. She was afraid of what was happening to her. There was no other reason.

She startled when gentle hands held her shoulders. "What's happening, Martha? What can I do to help?" Martha turned to face Joel. He was always there when she needed him.

She shook her head. "I…" What did she tell him? She felt like a fool. There was nothing wrong with her, she was sure of it. Only her mind playing tricks. The door to the church opened and Doc Ryan came out. This was turning into a circus. "I'm alright," she gasped, her breathing labored.

"I'll be the judge of that," the doc said, then sat her down. "Take a breath in and slowly let it out."

Martha did as she was told.

"And again." He listened carefully. "Keep going." After repeating this same thing for nearly a minute, she felt a lot better. "You can stop now," he told her.

"What's going on?" Joel asked, concern covering his face.

Doc Ryan ran a hand across his chin. "I'm not really sure, but I think it was a panic attack. Martha was hyperventilating, making her breathless." He turned to Martha then. "Do you want to talk about it?"

Everything he said rang true, but she had no intention of discussing why it happened. Especially with Joel standing there, listening. "There's nothing to talk about," she said, not being entirely truthful, but not lying either. She had no wish to speak about her feelings to either man. She was a mature-aged woman having silly teenage thoughts. How did she explain that?

Joel sat down next to her. "I'll stay with her," he told the doc. "If things change, I'll come and get you. I promise," he said when Doc Ryan opened his mouth, presumably to object.

"Alright, but make sure you do," he told Joel firmly. He stood then, and went back into the church, looking back over his shoulder as he did so.

The moment he was out of sight, Joel turned toward her. "What was that about?" he asked gently. "It's not like you to panic over anything, let alone while sitting in church." He reached out and took her hands. It was comforting, and Martha leaned into him. Sitting there with Joel, the world seemed alright again. As though *he* made everything right.

Of course, that was a silly notion. She was the one pushing away from him, not the other way around. It was then it hit her—she'd hurt his feelings. That's why he'd sat away from her. "I didn't mean…" She bit her lip then. How did she say it? Joel was her soulmate. She knew he was, but she still wasn't sure about moving forward with a relationship. That sounded like something a teenager would say. She certainly couldn't tell him that.

Martha tilted her head and glanced up at him. "I'm alright now," she whispered. And she was. The doc must have been right—she'd hyperventilated. She'd panicked over Joel keeping his distance although it was her who had pushed him away.

He stared at her. "We can wait out here until the service is over, if you like." His arm went up around her, and Martha felt comforted. She probably felt too comfortable, but she had no intention of pushing him away again.

"Maybe a few more minutes? I think I'll be fine to go back inside then." She fidgeted with her hands in her lap, couldn't keep them still. She was nervous. She knew she was. How silly for a woman of her age to feel nervous. She was with the one person she truly wanted to be with, the man she loved with all her heart.

And yet, something about the entire situation felt wrong. She did not know what it was. No matter, they would go back inside soon. She would join Wyatt again, and Joel would no doubt sit at the back of the church once again. Martha closed her eyes momentarily. *Please, God, help me through this dilemma.*

"I think I'm ready now," she told Joel, then stood.

He stood with her, his arm still around her waist, supporting her. "I'm right here by your side. I always will be," he said firmly. His words were reassuring and exactly what she needed to hear. He led her back inside, but guided her to the pew he'd been sitting on. They were at the very back of the church, away from prying eyes. It was exactly where she needed to be—with Joel by her side.

Sitting in the church hall, sipping tea, Martha felt normal again. Given the choice, she would have gone straight home, but the parishioners were concerned for her. It was the least she could do to ease their minds.

"Martha felt unwell," Joel said, when Mrs. Hargreaves voiced her concern. "Fresh air helped." She was grateful for his intervention. She'd already warded off several worried church-goers. Preacher Walters sat with her for a few minutes, ensuring all was well. She assured him she was. Joel's hand slipped into hers. He gently squeezed it, and a shiver ran through her. Why she continued to push him away, Martha wasn't sure.

If she was truthful with herself, in the back of her mind, she was certain she knew. Their break up had shattered her. It was mutual—the pair had become sick and tired of Dennis forever interfering. He constantly told them they should marry, and in the end, they'd had enough.

It wasn't like Dennis was married—he was a single man. Perhaps he should lead by example? Martha was certain it would never happen. Dennis liked to be alone. At least, that's what he told everyone. Whether or not he was lonely was a question for another time.

"Ah, Molly," Joel said, suddenly animated. Mrs. Cavendish was right behind her daughter. "Mrs. Cavendish. You remember Martha Cooley?"

Martha had little to do with the family as they lived on the outskirts of town, but she had seen them at church. They often left the moment the service was over. Usually because Mr. Cavendish was eager to get back home. She glanced about—he didn't seem to be here.

"Cookie?" Molly asked, pushing a plate toward Martha. She didn't care either way, but it would be impolite to refuse, especially since Molly had gone to the trouble.

"Thank you," she said, taking one of the smaller cookies from the plate. "How do you like working at the bakery?" Martha asked.

Molly's face lit up. "I adore it," she said with a smile on her face. "Joel is a good boss, too." Her cheeks colored, and Martha wondered what that was about. Did the young woman have a crush on Joel? She hoped not. Joel was far too old for her.

As though sensing an awkward pause coming up, Joel spoke. "Molly makes far better coffee than I do." He studied her momentarily. He opened his mouth to speak again, but closed it again. Was Molly's coffee better than hers? She doubted it. The special brew they made at the diner could not be replicated, since they mixed it themselves. One day she might share their secret with Joel, but not now.

Instead, she chuckled. "Anything would be better than your coffee." She bit her lip then. "Or so I've heard." She turned to Molly. "I'm sure your coffee is good. You should ensure the customers know about it."

Molly turned to Joel. "That's a great idea." He nodded.

Martha stood then. She was ready to go—this morning's incident had left her weary. All this small talk didn't help. "It's time for me to go," she said, unraveling her hand from Joel's. Molly's eyes watched the movement, then they opened wide in astonishment. She opened her mouth, but apparently thought better of it. Had she taken the job merely to get close to Joel? Did Molly think he was fair game?

The Joel she knew would not be interested in someone many years younger than himself. Besides, Joel had made his intent clear. He'd told Martha she was the only one for him. She knew he was right—Martha felt the same way. She knew what she had to do, even if it made her uncomfortable at times.

She had to open her heart to the man she loved and not back away.

Chapter Ten

Joel hooked his arm through Martha's. She still looked pale, but better than she did earlier. Was it his imagination, or did she sound… jealous talking to Molly? Surely not. Molly was almost half his age. Besides, he did not have romantic notions about the young woman. She was young enough to be his daughter, for goodness' sakes.

If that was really the way Martha felt, he would terminate Molly's employment. It was the last thing he wanted to do, because things were working out wonderfully. Molly was a quick learner and a hard worker. Since she'd begun working for him, Joel's life had become far easier. There was less pressure to do everything himself.

He shook himself mentally. This was all conjecture. Martha wasn't the jealous type. She never had been. "How are you feeling now?" he asked as they got closer to her cottage.

She turned to look at him. "A lot better, thank you."

Joel patted her hand. He was pleased. She had appeared terrified as she fled from the church, and he couldn't get to her quick enough. "Martha," he said slowly. "I know you're scared, but I…" Now she looked afraid. His words were not meant to frighten her. He stopped walking and stood in front of her. "Martha, neither of us is getting any younger. We're past our prime. At least I am."

She frowned. He stopped talking. Was he babbling like an idiot? No matter, he needed to continue. "I want to court you," he said in one long breath and through the tightness in his chest.

Her eyes opened in astonishment. Martha stared down at the ground for what seemed like an hour but was only moments in time. "I know," she whispered. Joel's heart pounded. His whole body stiffened waiting for her to answer. Seconds seemed to turn to minutes, and the minutes felt like hours. "That would be nice," she finally said, a smile on her face.

Was that a yes? Did Martha agree to let him court her? He would have asked her to marry him right now. They could turn around and go back to the church and beg Preacher Walters to marry them today. Except Joel knew Martha wouldn't agree. She would want her friends there. Especially Beth, and that was impossible given she'd only recently birthed little Rose.

Still, he was excited. Joel was convinced she would say no. But she didn't—she said yes! He was elated.

His heart felt as though it was pounding so hard it would leave his chest.

It was the first step to the rest of their lives. "Wonderful," he said excitedly. "How do you feel about a picnic?" He watched her every move, her every nuance.

"Today?" she asked, confused.

Joel thought that was clear. "Today. Now. We'll both be working tomorrow. I know it's short notice, but…"

"Yes," she said quickly and without hesitation. His heart filled with joy. Today it was.

Between them, they found enough food to make up a picnic. The bread was yesterday's, and the pie left over from last night's service at the diner, but they had plenty to fill their bellies. Besides, the quality of the food wasn't the point. This was about them courting.

Joel hired a horse and buggy from the livery so they could go further than the park up the road. He knew the hills like the back of his hand, although he'd not traveled up there for some time. Martha rarely went outside of town, and he hoped it would be a pleasant change for her.

He'd dug deep into the back of his closet and found a picnic blanket he hadn't used for some years. It was a little dusty, but would do nicely. There was a lovely spot near a stream, and he hoped it wasn't overtaken by foliage. He used to love going there, taking in the fresh air and the peacefulness of the area. Occasionally, he would drop a line in the stream and catch a fish or two.

He guided the horse into the spot he remembered from long ago and wasn't disappointed. It was still clear and accessible.

Joel climbed down from the buggy, then went around to Martha's side. She was already standing. Had she decided to climb down by herself? Not with him around! There was no way he'd allow that. If she lost her footing, she could be flat on her back. Or worse.

He cared for her far too much to allow that to happen.

Martha smiled as he stood beside the buggy, waiting to help her down. A flurry of warmth filled him because of a mere smile. That was the moment Joel knew he was deeply in love with Martha, and always had been. After all these years, his love had never waned.

"Let me help," he said gruffly. Her head shot up and her eyes pierced him. He didn't mean to sound so demanding, but he wasn't prepared to let her hear the emotion he knew his voice would hold.

"I can climb down by myself," she said teasingly, his gruffness seemingly forgotten.

Joel reached out his hands and took her by the waist. She was such a delicate creature. Not that he wasn't aware of the fact. He'd held Martha many a time, but that was before. When they courted the last time.

The memory filled him with heartache. Why, oh why, did he not force Dennis out of the picture? If he truly was a matchmaker, as Dennis claimed, he would ensure to keep them together, not tear the couple apart.

Joel shook his head. He was going over old ground. Dennis's failings were filling his mind instead of Martha. She needed to be his focus, and no one else. Nothing else. He lifted her carefully from the buggy. She stared down into his face. Her eyes sparkled in the sunlight, and she smiled at him again, then licked her lips.

It was almost his undoing.

He slowly brought her to the ground. Once she stood firmly next to him and Joel was certain she wouldn't fall, he pulled her close and wrapped his arms around her. Martha leaned her head on his shoulder. He breathed in her fragrance—lavender.

He knew it was her favorite, and had gifted her a bottle of lavender perfume the last time they courted.

Was this what she wore today? He felt heady. Holding her like this was only a fantasy yesterday. Today it was a dream come true. His heart fluttered, and he was filled with emotion. Pushing Martha away from himself, Joel stared into her face. "Martha, I…" No, he couldn't do it yet. If he asked her to marry him right at this moment, he was certain the answer would be no.

He promised to court her, and court her he would. Instead of making a fool of himself, he pulled her close and kissed his soulmate.

Chapter

Eleven

Martha's heart pounded.

With Joel's arms around her, she was exactly where she wanted to be. His warmth seeped into her, even in this slightly chilly cul-de-sac. Everything about this place was special. The quickly flowing stream filled her ears, the trees and other vegetation filled her senses. But most of all, Joel's unique fragrance filled her heart.

When he kissed her, Martha's knees almost buckled from under her. She felt weak as a newborn kitten. What was it about this man that set her heart aflutter? She would probably never know, but what she knew was she loved him. With all her heart. Martha wanted to spend the rest of her life with Joel Evans, and couldn't wait for that to happen.

They were courting, and that was a good first step.

She was anxious. Not because they were courting—she was elated about that. At least, she thought she was. This was not a first go-round for the pair, and that was the problem. Last time, they'd parted because of gossip. Dennis had done his part in pushing them together, and he'd spread the word.

Being a small town, word spread quickly. Far more quickly than wildfire. Therein was the problem. The resulting pressure was unsurmountable. Every person they met wanted to know when the wedding was scheduled. Who was making her dress, and when they were planning for children?

It was stress they didn't need. In the end, neither of them could cope with the gossip and everything that went with it. This time, they'd keep it quiet. Dennis was out of the equation. Right now, no one knew they were courting. Not even Beth.

It was hard to keep secrets from her best friend, but to be honest, when did she have the chance to tell her, anyway? Besides, who was Beth going to tell? She was bed bound and would be for sometime. Not that Beth was a gossip—far from it. Wyatt would never pass private information on to anyone, either.

"Martha? Are you alright? I'm moving too quickly, aren't I?" Joel stared into her face. He appeared remorseful.

"Not at all," she said, licking her lips. "I was just lost in my thoughts."

He smiled then, and her heart fluttered. A smile from Joel was what she lived for. Why, therefore, had she pushed him away for so long? Martha leaned into him again.

"We better get this picnic sorted," he suddenly said, moving her aside. Had he tired of her already? Martha knew better. Joel was an all-business kind of person. She learned last time they courted he had rituals he liked to follow, and she respected that. Being out of his comfort zone, as he would be here, would be difficult for him.

Martha knew it would have been a big deal for him to come up here with her. It was not part of his ritual. When they were courting last time, they would spend time together after the midday meal on Sundays, and part again for supper.

She respected his rituals then and would do it again now.

Joel removed the picnic basket from the buggy, along with the blanket. Martha stood at the end of the stream, watching the water flow. An occasional fish swam across in front of her, and she wondered if anyone ever came here to fish.

"I have caught the occasional fish here, but the fishing is far better further upstream," he said. "As you can see, the water is crystal clear here. It is there as well. It's so easy to catch fish there, it's almost criminal." He laughed then, and it sent her heart aflutter again. The sound of his voice was enough to send her heart into a spin. His laugh sent it soaring to heights she never thought possible.

All she wanted to do was hold him and be held by him. Martha watched as Joel spread the blanket over the damp ground, then set the basket down. She sat and emptied the basket. Along with the bread, she had left over roast chicken from the previous night and packed that as well. They certainly wouldn't go hungry, but if she was honest, Martha wasn't particularly hungry. She simply wanted to spend time with Joel.

The pair knew each other better than most. She also knew they were skirting around each other. Why had they bowed to pressure from others? It would have been far easier, and better, for them to have married.

It wasn't too late—that was the good news. The fact they'd lost over a year from their stubbornness, some would even say stupidity, was regrettable.

"Joel, why don't we…"

She didn't get to finish the words. He reached over and covered her hand. "Why don't we eat first, then we can talk? I'm starving." He grinned, and Martha wondered if he knew what she was about to say.

The time was now. She didn't want to wait any longer. Whether Joel would agree was a completely different story.

"The food was delicious," Joel said, rubbing his belly. "We are both excellent cooks!" He laughed again, and it filled Martha with warmth. She could listen to him all day. Whether that was talking or laughing, she didn't care.

Being near to Joel filled her with happiness. Right now, she felt a joy she hadn't experienced for a long time. Since they parted ways.

She leaned in and repacked the picnic basket. There was little left to put away, but it had to be done. Martha would far prefer to be in Joel's arms or by his side, than doing this menial task.

"Shall we go for a walk?" he asked when the picnic things were carefully stowed on the buggy. "There's a bit of a path through there," he said, pointing through the trees. "It's not much, and it's not official. It's been made by visitors like us walking through the area."

"Why not?" Why not indeed? Joel seemed to know the area, and if they didn't wander far, they wouldn't get lost. At least she hoped not.

"Let me give the horse some oats before we leave." He walked over to the horse he'd tethered when they arrived and attached a bag of oats. "All set," he said a short time later. Then he hooked his arm through hers.

They stepped in between the large trees that overhung the dense bushland. "Are you sure it's safe?" she asked, feeling a little apprehensive.

Joel pulled her closer. "I'm positive. I used to come up here all the time."

He'd nearly brought her up here once. They had planned a picnic that time, too. Word got back to them about Dennis and his gossiping ways, foreseeing their wedding in the next weeks. That was the end of the line. Neither one could take it anymore and called it quits.

The pity of it was they truly loved each other. Why they allowed the town busybodies to tear them apart, Martha would never know. Beth had counseled her to ignore them. She truly wished she had.

As they strolled through the trees, beautiful sounds permeated her senses. She stopped to listen. "What is that?" she asked Joel, tipping her head skyward.

He smiled, and it lit up his face. "I can hear a magpie, and perhaps a wren or two," he said.

She listened again. "I think I can hear a warbler, too. Oh Joel," she said, squeezing his hand. "It truly is wonderful here. I could spend forever here." She turned to face him. "Provided it was with you."

At first, he frowned. Did he think she meant for protection? That was far from what she meant. Anywhere Martha spent with Joel was special. Magical even.

Suddenly, he leaned in and kissed her. His arms went up around her, and he held her close. "I never want to lose you again," he whispered in her ear. "I love you with all my heart."

Tears sprung from her eyes. "I love you too," she said, then kissed him again.

Chapter

Twelve

They were mostly silent on the way home. Likely because the words that really mattered had already been said. *I love you* had been on his lips for far too long. He wondered if that was the same for Martha. Had she wanted to utter the words and been afraid?

He had certainly been fearful of saying them. Joel didn't want her to run from him again. Martha was a strong woman, but could also be flighty. She was impulsive too, which was the complete opposite of him. It had taken all Joel's effort to ask her to the picnic today. He didn't do the last minute well.

Everything needed to be planned, and he had to work out every detail. It was surprising, given his idiosyncrasies, she hadn't run long ago. He'd been that way as long as he could remember, and it had served him well. Martha had not once demanded he stop, and he loved her all the more because of it.

"What now?" he found himself saying.

"I don't understand," she said as she faced him, and was frowning.

Had he confused her? Worried her? Neither was what he'd intended. He pulled to the side of the road, ensuring the buggy was stable. He slid sideways in his seat and took her hand. "We've established we love each other," he said quietly. "I've loved you for far more years than you probably understand." His heart thudded at the regrets. So many years had passed where Martha was untouchable. Married to another man meant he kept his distance.

Once that man met his demise, everything changed. There had to be a respectable mourning period, of course. By then he was set in his ways, and Martha likely was too. He let things slide. But not again.

He stared into Martha's gentle face, her eyes now wide with astonishment. "Martha Cooley," he said quietly, "I don't want to lose another day with you." He dropped to one knee, which wasn't easy, given he was still on the buggy. He drew in a huge breath before saying the words. "Will you marry me?"

"I will," she said as she screwed up her face, trying not to cry. He reached up and brushed away the tears that slid down her face.

He sat down again and took her in his arms. Joel had not planned to ask her today, but his heart told him now was the time. Tomorrow, they would start planning a wedding. Planning was what he did best.

Joel heard Wyatt's voice coming from the bakery. He was in his favorite place—the kitchen. This was where he felt most comfortable. Everything had a place, and he knew exactly where that was. His utensils never let him down, and neither did his ingredients. It sounded silly, even to Joel, but his mind worked in a certain way, and he had accepted the situation a long time again.

He brushed his flour covered hands on his apron and hurried out to the store. "Good morning," he told Wyatt. "Coffee?"

Wyatt studied him. "I hadn't planned on staying." He continued to study his friend.

"Molly, two coffees, if you wouldn't mind." He then guided Wyatt to a table where they both sat down. Wyatt studied him curiously.

His shop assistant glanced at him curiously. It wasn't often Joel veered away from his normal ritual. Molly was becoming used to him now, and he to her. She made his life far easier, and she enjoyed being employed. It worked for them both.

"Would you like a pastry with your coffee?" he asked Wyatt, then stood.

Wyatt's face tensed. "What's wrong? Something is wrong, I can tell."

Molly placed the coffee in front of them. "Find a nice pastry for Wyatt, if you will," he said as he sat down again. He waved Molly away, but she was back in a matter of moments.

A customer entered the store and Molly busied herself with the woman. It was good. He wanted to spend time with his friend. Joel took a sip of coffee. "Molly's coffee is far better than mine," he said.

"You're not wrong there," Wyatt told him, a smirk on his face. "What's this all about?" he asked, serious again, then took a bite of the custard-filled pastry. "You've outdone yourself with this one, my friend," he said, wiping his mouth with the napkin Molly supplied.

Joel couldn't help but grin. "There's a surprise in the center," he said as he raised his eyebrows.

Wyatt took another bite. "Delicious. Who but Joel Evans, baker extraordinaire, would think to put blueberries in the center of a custard pastry?" He wiped his mouth again.

Wyatt finished the pastry, his eyes never leaving Joel. "Am I the guinea pig again? Trying your new creations?"

"Nothing like that," Joel said. "I'm just happy to see you." Joel drained his mug of coffee, then stood. "I better get back to it."

Wyatt studied him. "Something is up. You're not yourself." He pierced Joel with his eyes.

Joel grinned. "You'll find out soon enough. Molly," he said, turning to the assistant. "Pack three pastries for Wyatt, compliments of the house."

He turned then and went back to his kitchen, whistling as he did so. He felt Wyatt's eyes on his back the entire time. Joel promised not to tell anyone until Martha told Beth, and he'd kept that promise.

Wyatt would find out the moment he arrived home, he was certain.

Martha sat on the side of Beth's bed as the new mother breastfed baby Rose.

One day, if she was lucky, that could be her. It was then it occurred to Martha it was not something she had discussed with Joel. Not that it was a decent conversation for an unmarried woman to have with a single gent. The mere thought put heat in her face.

"What are you thinking?" Beth asked, a hint of laughter in her voice. "Your cheeks are suddenly pink."

Martha slapped her hands to her face, then shook her head. "Nothing," she said, training her eyes on the babe to avoid her friend's scrutiny. "That's not true," she admitted, not able to hide the news any longer. "I have something to tell you." She smiled then, and excitement grew inside her, the way it had when Joel had asked her to marry him.

Beth watched her carefully, not saying a word. It was disconcerting. Finally, Beth spoke. "Do I have to pry it out of you? I am rather tied down at the moment." She glanced down at the tiny baby and ran a gentle finger down her cheek.

"But by the Grace of God," Martha murmured, and Beth's head shot up. A huge smile covered her face.

"You can't do that to me," Beth said. "Tell me now!"

Martha wiggled on the side of the bed to get more comfortable. "Joel asked me to marry him! We're getting married!" She almost squealed but remembered little Rose in time. The last thing she wanted was to scare her tiny goddaughter.

Beth's eyes opened wide. "Oh, Martha, I am so happy for you both. If I didn't have Rose hanging off a breast, I would hug you right now."

"I'll hug you instead," Martha said, and leaned in and gave her friend a side hug, ensuring she didn't disturb the baby. When she pulled away, there were tears in Beth's eyes. It was all Martha could do not to cry as well. "Look at us," she said. "Crying out of happiness." She wiped a stray tear from her eyes.

The sound of the front door opening, then closing, alerted them Wyatt was home. He glanced across at them from the doorway. "Right," he said. "I knew something was up—I've just seen Joel."

"He didn't tell you?" Martha asked, trying not to smirk.

"Point blank refused." Wyatt didn't appear annoyed, more curious. He glanced from one woman to the other. "Someone tell me, for goodness' sakes," he demanded, which was unlike Wyatt. Perhaps he thought the news was bad.

Martha stood. "Joel asked me to marry him. I said yes," she said far more calmly than she felt. She didn't think she would ever marry again, but knew Joel was the right person. When she lost Harry all those years ago, she vowed not to remarry. The heartache was far too much to bear. But things change. People change, and that had been proven.

Her soulmate, the man she'd loved from afar for way too long, wanted to spend forever with her. And she with him.

Wyatt stepped forward and wrapped his arms around her. "It's about time," he said, right before he dropped his arms. Martha couldn't help but see the grin on his face.

"There is no way I am missing this wedding!" Beth declared as she helped Martha dress for her wedding.

"It's only three weeks since you birthed Rose," Martha said, knowing she was fighting a losing battle. She had discussed the date with Beth and wanted to put it off further. Beth was convinced if it was any later, the pair would change their minds. The way they had in the past.

The difference this time was the secrecy involved.

They'd kept the news between only a handful of people and sworn them to secrecy. If Dennis had been included, the matchmaker would have spread the news about town. It was their downfall last time around, and neither Joel nor Martha were prepared to take the risk.

Martha had been preparing for this day, along with Joel. They were keeping it to a small affair with a small luncheon afterwards. Between the happy couple and Allie, there was plenty to feed their guests. The diner was closed for the day, so it would be a private meal as well.

The only way they'd managed that was through their ring of confidentiality. Normally, everyone from town would attend weddings, but an intimate setting is what they preferred. They were private people, after all.

Martha smiled at what she believed would be Dennis's reaction when he found out. Hopefully not until after the ceremony. As the town matchmaker, he believed he should attend every wedding, but

Martha was convinced it was only so he could bask in what he believed was the glory of a job well done.

The thought made her laugh out loud. "Poor Dennis," she said, and Beth waved a hand across in front of her.

"Dennis gets what Dennis deserves. He tore you two apart last time. Without his interference, you would have married long ago." Beth seemed wistful then. "You may even have had a babe or two."

She was right, of course she was. But this time, the pair had stayed clear of the matchmaker. He meant well, of course, but sometimes went overboard. It didn't bode well with her, and Joel was furious with the man. He definitely didn't want him at the wedding. He'd even stopped supplying the mercantile with pastries. Dennis seemed to be at a loss to understand why.

"Time to leave," Beth said, breaking into Martha's reflections. "You look beautiful," she whispered, her voice full of emotion. She pulled Martha in for a hug, and the pair stood silently for what seemed forever.

"Joel will be waiting," Martha finally whispered, but Beth still held her tight.

"He'll wait," Beth said, and Martha was certain she was crying. Suddenly, she pushed Martha away. "I'm so happy for you both. It's a match made in heaven," she said as tears streamed down her face. "We are both stubborn. Look how much time Wyatt and I wasted." She shook her head then. "And here's me, wasting more of the time you'll have together. We need to go." She grabbed Martha by the hand and led her out of the house and toward the church.

Martha smiled when she noticed Dennis standing in the doorway to the mercantile, gawking.

Epilogue

Eight and a half months later…

Martha stirred the soup, then lined the biscuits up on the tray, ready to be cooked. She leaned down and opened the oven door. That's when it happened. She slammed the oven door closed again, then hurried into the dining room and sat tentatively on a chair. Allie ran to her side.

"Did you spill something in the kitchen, or…?" She left the question hanging when she glanced into Martha's face. "I guess it's or. I'll get Joel." Soon she was alone.

Her wonderful husband had tried to get her to stop working, but he always knew Martha wanted to work right up until she could no longer do it. He was such a caring man, and she couldn't fault him.

She wasn't gone long, but the moment Allie returned, Martha began barking out orders. "Give the soup another stir, Allie. The biscuits are ready to go into the oven. And the roast—you know what to do," she said as she winced.

Martha glanced up as the diner door opened. Joel strode inside, followed by Doctor Marcus Ryan. "Can you stand?" the doc asked as Joel wrapped his arms around her.

She glanced up into the doctor's face. "My water's broke," she said on a sob. "It's too early."

Joel gazed at the doc, who hastened to reassure them both. "Not for twins, it isn't," he said. "Let's get you home and comfortable."

The two men lifted her from the chair and near carried Martha home. She would soon be a mother—a lifelong dream she never thought would come to fruition.

Joel hurried into the bedroom the moment the doc opened the door. He was white as a ghost. Martha knew he'd been worried about her, but hadn't understood the full impact of his concern. She was concerned *he* needed a doctor more than she did.

He stood beside the bed, staring down at her with the two babes in her arms—one at each breast. Joel had tears in his eyes, much like herself. "Our miracle babies," he whispered. "And my beautiful wife. I love you with all my heart," he said, then dropped to his knees beside the bed. Joel leaned in and kissed her gently, then reached out to touch each baby, but pulled back.

"They won't break," she said, laughter in her voice.

He studied her then. "I know, but a man can't be too careful."

Suddenly one of the babies, Alexander, began to wail. "Do you want to hold him?" Martha asked.

Joel floundered. "I…" He screwed up his face a little before answering. "Should I?"

Martha laughed. "You are their father," she said. Had he forgotten that already?

Joel stood and straightened his shoulders. "I am indeed," then reached for the crying baby. "Is this Alexander or Petunia?" he asked, clearly confused.

Smiling, Martha answered. "This is Alexander. I have no doubt he'll become your baker's apprentice in the years to come."

Beaming, Joel took the baby and held him close to his heart. Alexander stopped wailing almost instantly. It was as though he knew he was safely cradled in his father's arms.

Martha knew life would never be the same, nor did she want it to be.

From the Author

Thank you so much for reading my book – I hope you enjoyed it.

I would greatly appreciate you leaving a review where you purchased, even if it is only a one-liner. It helps to have my books more visible!

~*~

About the Author

Multi-published, award-winning and bestselling author Cheryl Wright, former secretary, debt collector, account manager, writing coach, and shopping tour hostess, loves reading.

She writes both historical and contemporary western romance, as well as romantic suspense.

She lives in Melbourne, Australia, and is married with two adult children and has six grandchildren. When she's not writing, she can be found in her craft room making greeting cards.

Links

Website: *http://www.cheryl-wright.com/*

Facebook Reader Group:
https://www.facebook.com/groups/cherylwrightaut hor/

Join My Newsletter:

https://cheryl-wright.com/newsletter/
(and receive a free book)

www.ingramcontent.com/pod-product-compliance
Lightning Source LLC
Chambersburg PA
CBHW070625120726
47909CB00004B/1333